Mouse's Halloween Party

Mouse's Halloween Party

by Jeanne Modesitt
Illustrated by Robin Spowart

Boyds Mills Press

Published by Boyds Mills Press
815 Church Street
Honesdale, Pennsylvania 18431
Printed in China

Library of Congress Cataloging-in-Publication Data

Modesitt, Jeanne.
Mouse's Halloween party / by Jeanne Modesitt ; illustrated by Robin Spowart. — 1st ed.
32 p. : col. ill. ; cm.
ISBN 1563979500 (alk. paper)
1. Halloween — Fiction. 2. Mice — Fiction. I. Spowart, Robin, ill. II. Title
[E] 21   PZ7.M634Mo   2004
LC Control Number: 2001094575

First edition, 2004
The text of this book is set in 15-point Optima.

Visit our Web site at www.boydsmillspress.com

10 9 8 7 6 5 4 3 2 1

To Zoë and Zach,
we love you
—J. M. and R. S.

It was the day before Halloween, and Mouse was very excited.

He had just asked Mama if he could have a Halloween party tomorrow, and Mama had said yes.

Mouse danced on one foot. His party was going to be the best Halloween party in the world!

"Can I invite Hedgehog?" Mouse asked Mama.

"Of course," said Mama.

"And Squirrel?"

"Absolutely."

"And Bunny and Mole and Pig?"

Mama smiled. "You can invite them all," she said.

Mouse jumped in the air. "Yippee!" he said.

The next step was to go see his friends and invite them to the party.

Mouse put on his Halloween costume and skipped out the door.

His first stop was Hedgehog's house.

Mouse knocked on the door, and Hedgehog and his papa opened it.

"Can you come to my house tomorrow at four o'clock?" asked Mouse. "I'm going to have a Halloween party."

Hedgehog looked up at his papa. "Can I, Papa?" he asked.

Hedgehog's papa nodded. "Sounds fine to me," he said.

Hedgehog turned to Mouse and smiled. "I can go," he said.

"Good!" said Mouse. "See you tomorrow. Bye!"

Next, Mouse went to Squirrel's house, then Bunny's, then Mole's. All three said yes, they would love to come to Mouse's Halloween party.

"Good!" said Mouse to each of them. "See you tomorrow."

Finally, Mouse arrived at Pig's house. Mouse knocked on the door, and Pig and her mama opened it.

"Guess what?" said Mouse to Pig. "I'm having a Halloween party tomorow at four o'clock, and Hedgehog and Squirrel and Bunny and Mole are all coming. Can you come, too? There will be lots of games, and my mama is making Halloween cupcakes."

But instead of saying yes, Pig started to cry.

Mouse's eyes opened wide. "Pig, what's the matter? Don't you like Halloween parties?"

Pig's mama put her arms around Pig. "Pig, do you want to tell Mouse why you're crying?"

Pig turned to Mouse, her cheeks wet with tears.
" I . . . I was going to have a Halloween party
tomorrow, too," she said.

A look of surprise came over Mouse's face.
"You were?" he said.

Pig nodded. Two big tears fell from her eyes.
"I . . . I was going to invite Hedgehog and Squirrel
and Bunny and Mole and you. I even made everyone
Halloween presents. And Mama made Halloween
cookies. It was going to be the best Halloween party
in the world." And with that, Pig let out a fresh burst of
sobs and ran from the door into her room.

Pig's mama patted Mouse's head. "Don't worry,"
she said. "It's not your fault that Pig is so upset. Maybe
she can have a Halloween party next year." And she
said good-bye to Mouse and closed the door.

Mouse turned away from the door. He felt sad that Pig was crying. He walked home and told Mama what had happened. When he finished, Mama kissed him.

"I'm sorry Pig is so sad," she said.

Mouse sighed. "Me, too," he said.

Mouse leaned against Mama for a minute, then said, "I think I'll go outside and swing for a while." He walked into the backyard, sat down on the swing, and pushed himself off the ground.

Back and forth, he swung.
Back and forth . . .
Then, all of a sudden, Mouse came to a stop.
He jumped off the swing, ran inside the house,
and called out, "Mama! Mama! I've got an idea!"

Later, Mouse was again knocking on Pig's door.

Pig and her mama opened the door. Pig's eyes were red from crying, and she was sniffling.

Mouse danced on one foot. He was very excited. "Pig!" he said. "I've got a great idea! You and I could have a Halloween party *together*."

Pig stopped sniffing. "Together?" she asked.

"Yes," said Mouse. "We could invite Hedgehog and Squirrel and Bunny and Mole to a Halloween party at the park tomorrow. I'll bring my games and my mama's Halloween cupcakes, and you can bring your presents and your mama's Halloween cookies. What do you think?"

A wide smile filled Pig's face. "I think that sounds great!" she said.

"Good!" said Mouse. "You want to come with me and tell everyone about our party?"

Pig looked up at her mama. Mama smiled down at Pig. "Go ahead, Pig," she said.

Pig reached out to take Mouse's hand. "Come on, Mouse," she said. "Let's go."

And off the two friends went, to invite Hedgehog and Squirrel and Bunny and Mole to the best Halloween party in the world.

Here are a couple of Halloween party games that are great fun.

Find the Pumpkins

You will need:
orange construction paper,
    or white paper you color orange
pencil
black felt-tip marker or black crayon
scissors

With your pencil, draw several pumpkin shapes on your paper. Draw faces on the pumpkins with either a marker or crayon. Cut out the pumpkin shapes with scissors. On the backs of somel pumpkin shapes, draw a single star. Put these pumpkins aside. Take the rest of the shapes, and on the backs of some of them, draw two stars, and on the backs of others, draw three stars.

Next, ask a grown-up (who isn't going to play the game) to hide the pumpkins. (No one else can peek!) When the pumpkins are all hidden, ask the grown-up to tell everyone, "Okay, go find the pumpkins!" When all the pumpkins have been found (or when everyone has given up looking), everyone counts the stars on his or her pumpkins. The person who has the greatest number of stars wins!

Pin the Nose on the Pumpkin

You will need:
white paper
black felt-tip marker or black crayon
orange crayon (optional)
tape
scissors
double-sided tape
blindfold

With a black marker or crayon, draw a large pumpkin on a piece of white paper. Draw eyes and a mouth, but do not draw a nose. If you would like, you can color the eyes and mouth black, and the rest of the pumpkin orange. Ask a grown-up to hang the drawing on the wall.

Now you need to draw some noses! On white paper, draw several noses, the same size and shape. (Each player gets a nose, so draw enough noses to go around.) Cut out the noses. On the front of each nose, write a number (a different number for each player). On the back of each nose, put a small piece of double-sided tape. Hand each player a nose.

Blindfold each player as he or she takes a turn to play. Spin each player around a few times and then let him or her go (pointing the player in the right direction, of course!). Each player must try to tape his or her pumpkin nose on the pumpkin in the correct spot. Other kids can yell "hot" if the player is close to the correct spot, or "cold" if the player is way off. The player who comes closest to the right spot is the winner.